# Mr Little's
# NOISY PLANE

## Richard Fowler

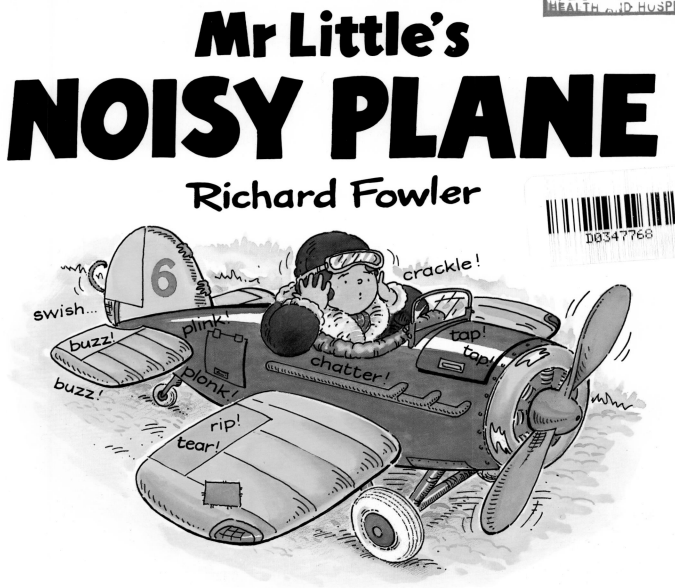

LITTLE
MAMMOTH

Mr Little was getting ready
to fly his plane in the
local air show, when
he heard a tapping noise
coming from inside.
"I wonder what that can be,"
said Mr Little, lifting the
engine cowling . . .

Elevator

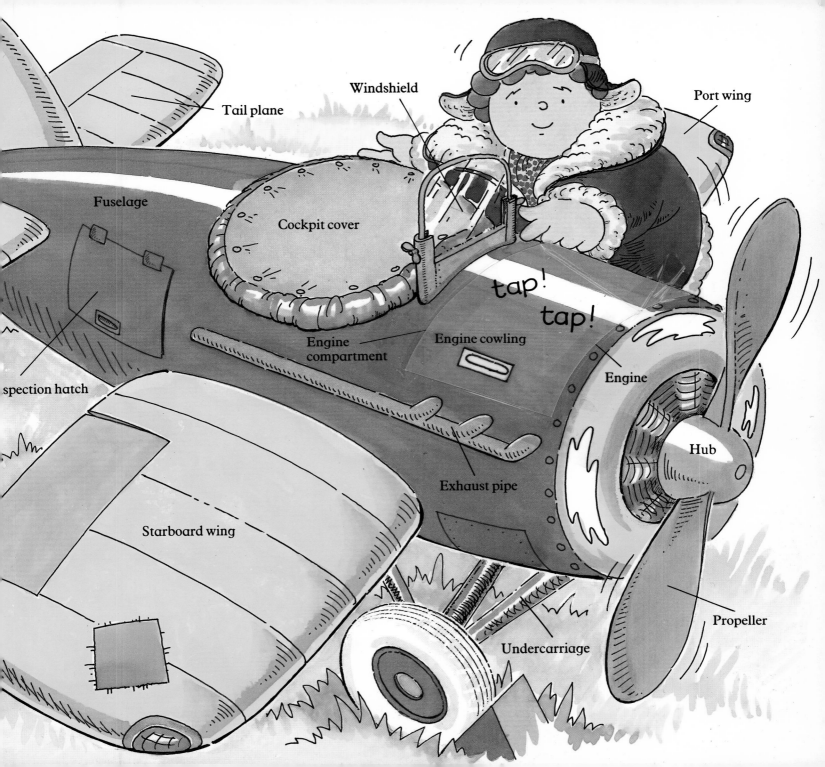

A ripping and tearing sound came from under the right-hand wing. "Oh, no! What now?" sighed Mr Little. He looked under the flap and found . . .

Tail wheel

Flying jacket

Parachute

A plink-plonk, plink-plonk sound came from inside the fuselage. "I'll bet that's another mouse," said Mr Little, as he climbed over the tail plane to lift the inspection hatch.

Rudder

Flying boots

Elevator

Tail fin

6

Inspection hatch

plink!

plonk!

plink!

plonk!

Control cables

Tail plane

Crackling and
chattering noises came
from inside the cockpit.
"Must be air traffic control
on the radio,"
said Mr Little,
as he took off
the cockpit cover.

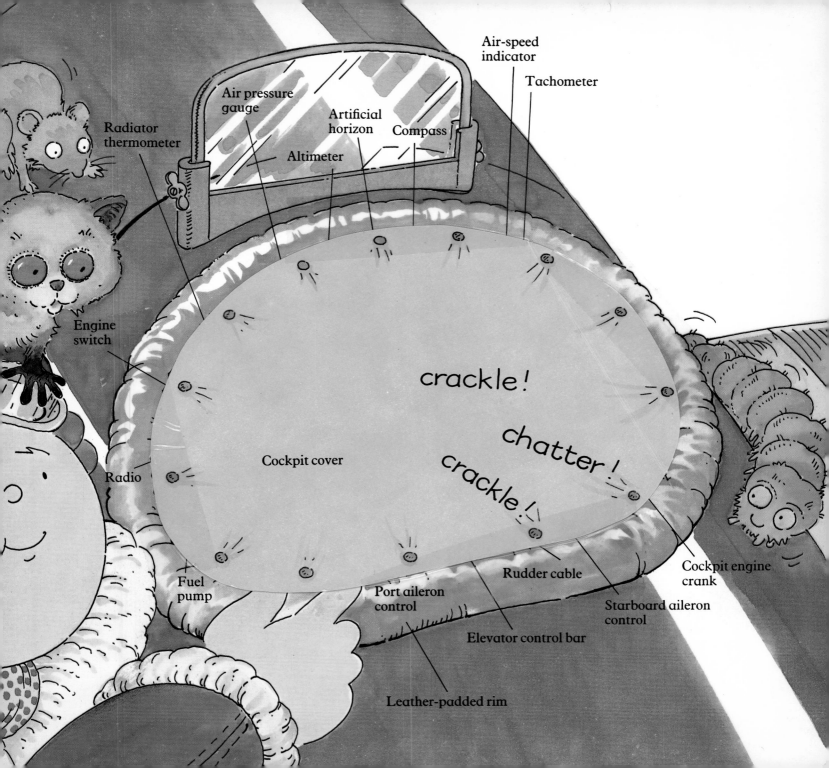

"I'll never get off the ground at this rate," moaned Mr Little, when he heard a swishing sound coming from the rear of the plane.

Map case

"Will plane number six please
hurry up and get ready
for takeoff!" said a voice
over the loudspeaker.
"Keep your wings on!"
shouted Mr Little,
as he heard a buzzing sound
coming from under the plane.
He lifted the
right elevator . . .

Rudder

Fuselage

Tail plane

Elevator

buzz!

buzz!

"Eeeeek, I'm off!"
yelled Mr Little,
jumping into the cockpit.
The mouse, the caterpillar,
the bush baby,
the cockatoo,
and the monkey
all hung on as the plane
raced down the runway . . .

Control tower

Hangar

ind sock

Cloud

Airfield

Runway

and with a tap, a rip, a tear,
a plink-plonk, a crackle,
a chatter, a swish, a buzz
and a very loud . . .